One Little Kitten

by Tana Hoban

Greenwillow Books, New York

Published by Greenwillow Books
A Division of William Morrow & Company, Inc.
105 Madison Avenue, New York, N.Y. 10016
Printed in the United States of America
First Edition

10 9 8 7 6 5 4 3 2 1

Design by Ava Weiss

Library of Congress
Cataloging in Publication Data
Hoban, Tana.   One little kitten.
Summary: Brief rhyming text and photographs
follow a kitten as it explores its surroundings.
[1. Cats — Fiction. 2. Stories in rhyme]
I. Title. PZ8.3.H65170n [E] 78-31862
ISBN 0-688-80222-2   ISBN 0-688-84222-4 lib. bdg.

This one is for Max

A new day !

It's time to play.

A place to hide

inside.

Where to?

Through.

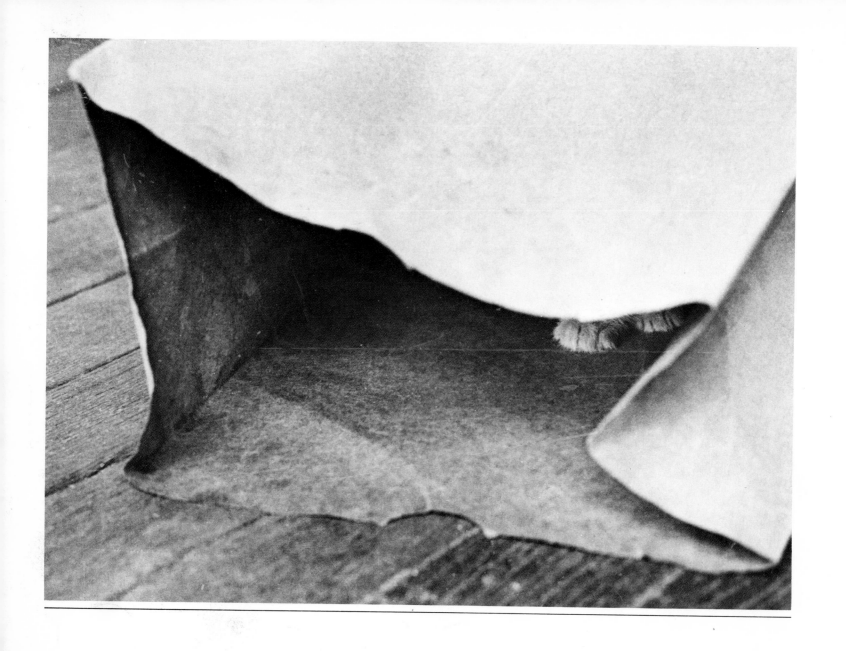

I'll disappear

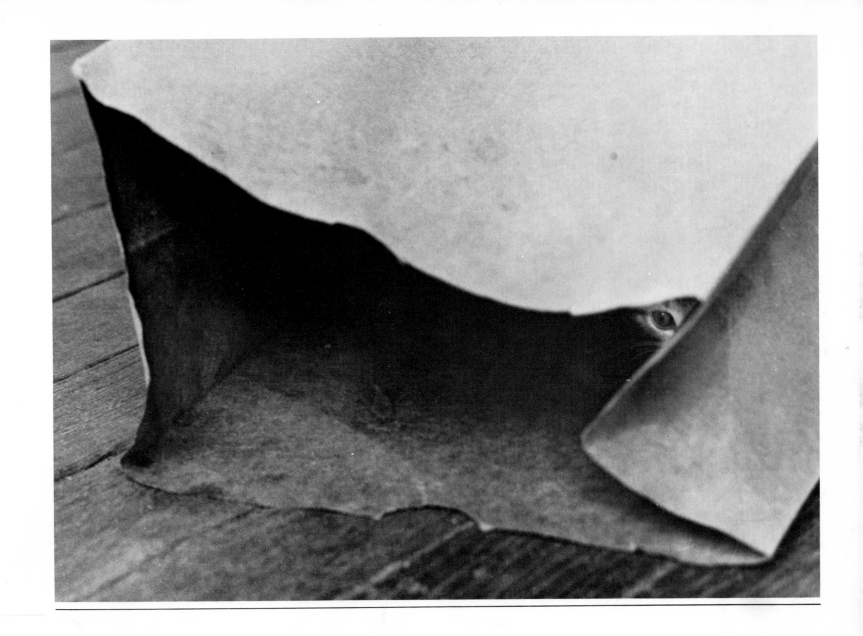

and

come out here.

Is there room

behind this broom?

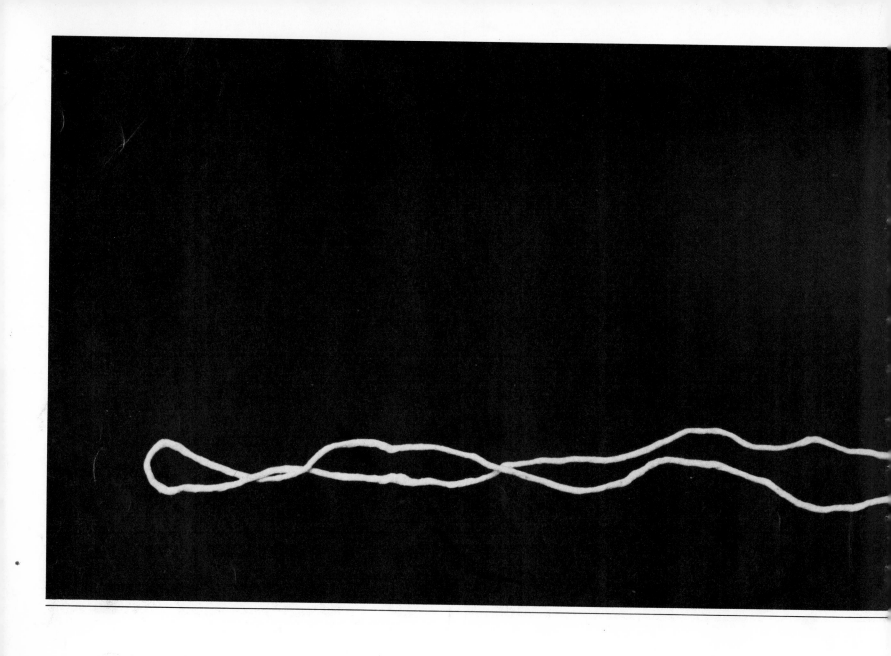

Just the thing —

string!

A funny place

to put my face.

It's getting late.

Will they wait?

Hug me tight.

Good night—

Good night.